Brownilocks

and the
Three Bowls of Cornflakes

Written by Enid Richemont

Illustrated by Polona Lovšin

Crabtree Publishing Company

www.crabtreebooks.com

Crabtree Publishing Company
www.crabtreebooks.com
1-800-387-7650

PMB 59051,
350 Fifth Ave., 59th Floor
New York, NY 10118

616 Welland Ave.
St. Catharines, ON
L2M 5V6

Published by Crabtree Publishing in 2016

Series editor: Melanie Palmer
Series designer: Peter Scoulding
Series advisor: Catherine Glavina
Editor: Petrice Custance
Notes to adults: Reagan Miller
Prepress technician: Ken Wright
Print production coordinator: Margaret Amy Salter

Text © Enid Richemont 2010
Illustration © Polona Lovšin 2010

Printed in Canada/012016/BF20151123

First published in 2010 by Wayland (A division of Hachette Children's Books)

Library and Archives Canada
Cataloguing in Publication

Richemont, Enid, author
      Brownilocks and the three bowls of cornflakes
/ written by Enid Richemont ; illustrated by Polona
Lovsin.

(Tadpoles fairytale twists)
Issued in print and electronic formats.
ISBN 978-0-7787-2459-9 (bound).--
ISBN 978-0-7787-2511-4 (paperback).--
ISBN 978-1-4271-7720-9 (html)

      I. Lovsin, Polona, illustrator II. Title. III.
Series: Tadpoles. Fairytale twists

PZ7.R393Br 2016   j823'.914   C2015-907109-7
                                        C2015-907110-0

Library of Congress
Cataloging-in-Publication Data

CIP available at Library of Congress

This story is based on the traditional fairy tale,
Goldilocks and the Three Bears, but with a new twist.
Can you make up your own twist for the story?

Mom put out three
bowls of cornflakes.

"Let's go for a walk before breakfast," she said.

Brownilocks the bear was out walking, too. She smelled the cornflakes. "M-m-m, tasty," she thought, climbing in.

Brownilocks sat
on Dad's chair.
"Too hard!"
she growled.

So she tried
Mom's chair.
"Too soft!"
she moaned.

She went over to Sam's chair.
"Just right!" she thought,
reaching for Sam's cornflakes.

But ... CRASH!
Brownilocks was too
heavy and Sam's
chair snapped.

Brownilocks felt
sleepy. She tried
the biggest bed.
"Too hard!"
she grunted.

She tried the next bed.
"Too bouncy!"
she cried.

Then she tried the smallest bed.
"Just right!" she said, so she
climbed on and fell
fast asleep.

Mom, Dad, and Sam came back
from their walk. Dad frowned.
"Who's been sitting in my chair?"
he asked.

"Who's been sitting in my chair?"
Mom gasped. Then Sam yelled,
"Who broke my chair and
ate all my cornflakes?"

They looked all over the house.
"Who's been sleeping in my
bed?" cried Dad.
"And in my bed!" cried Mom.

"Hey! Look who's in my bed!"
yelled Sam. "And she's snoring!"

Brownilocks woke up,
rushed downstairs, and ran
outside. She ran across the
garden and into the woods.

"She was a nice bear,"
Sam sighed.
"I wish she'd come back."

Dad fixed Sam's chair
and found a bean bag
for Brownilocks.

The next morning, Mom put out four bowls of cornflakes—one for her, one for Sam, one for Dad, and a big one for the bear.

Brownilocks soon came back
when she smelled the cornflakes.

"Here's your bowl," said Sam.

"Here's your bean bag," called Dad.

Brownilocks sat on Dad's chair.

"Try the bean bag," Dad said.

Then Brownilocks tried Sam's bowl.

"This one's bigger!"
said Sam.

Brownilocks gobbled up all the
cornflakes and slurped up
all the milk in the big bowl.

Brownilocks yawned. She thumped up the stairs and lay on Sam's bed.

Then Sam curled up with
Brownilocks and read her a story.

But Brownilocks longed to be
outside. She climbed out of
the window and ran
into the woods.

Sam wanted to see his new friend again. "Come back soon!" he cried.

Brownilocks liked the woods,
but she also liked Sam—and
the tasty cornflakes.

She did come back the very next
day, and the day after that,
and the day after that!

Puzzle 1

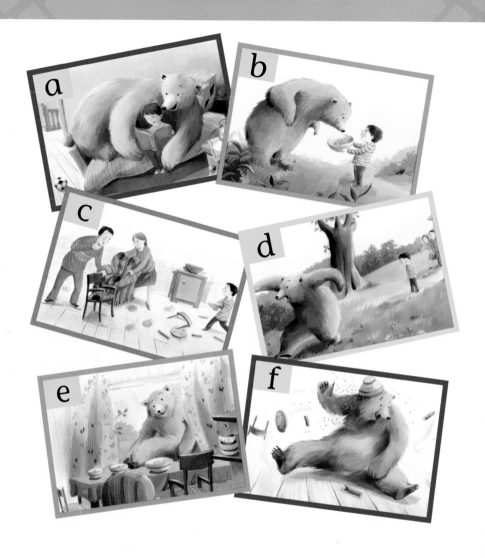

Put these pictures in the correct order. Which event do you think is the most important? Now try writing the story in your own words!

Puzzle 2

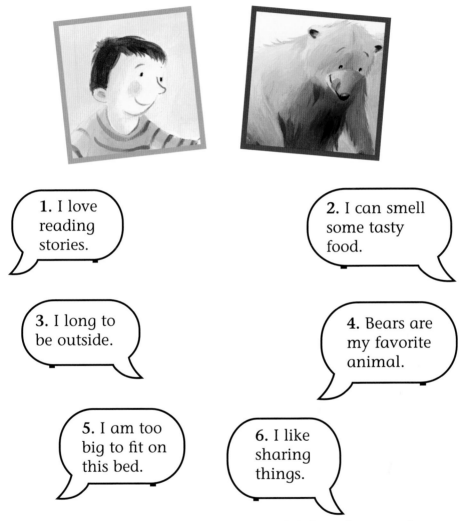

1. I love reading stories.

2. I can smell some tasty food.

3. I long to be outside.

4. Bears are my favorite animal.

5. I am too big to fit on this bed.

6. I like sharing things.

Choose the correct speech bubbles for each character. Can you think of any others? Turn the page to find the answers for both puzzles.

Notes for Adults

TADPOLES: **Fairytale Twists** are engaging, imaginative stories designed for early fluent readers. The books may also be used for read-alouds or shared reading with young children.

TADPOLES: **Fairytale Twists** are humorous stories with a unique twist on traditional fairy tales. Each story can be compared to the original fairy tale, or appreciated on its own. Fairy tales are a key type of literary text found in the Common Core State Standards.

The following PROMPTS before, during, and after reading support literacy skill development and can enrich shared reading experiences:

1. **Before Reading:** Do a picture walk through the book, previewing the illustrations. Ask the reader to predict what will happen in the story. For example, ask the reader what he or she thinks the twist in the story will be.

2. **During Reading:** Encourage the reader to use context clues and illustrations to determine the meaning of unknown words or phrases.

3. **During Reading:** Have the reader stop midway through the book to revisit his or her predictions. Does the reader wish to change his or her predictions based on what they have read so far?

4. **During and After Reading:** Encourage the reader to make different connections:

   Text-to-Text: How is this story similar to/ different from other stories you have read?

   Text-to-World: How are events in this story similar to/different from things that happen in the real world?

   Text-to-Self: Does a character or event in this story remind you of anything in your own life?

5. **After Reading:** Encourage the child to reread the story and to retell it using his or her own words. Invite the child to use the illustrations as a guide.

Here are other titles from TADPOLES: Fairytale Twists for you to enjoy:

Answers
Puzzle 1
The correct order is: 1e, 2f, 3c, 4d, 5a, 6b
Puzzle 2
Sam: 1, 4, 6
Brownilocks: 2, 3, 5